I0841050

she is coming

She is Coming

Copyright © 2023 Penumbral Koi Publishing LLC

All rights reserved. Except as permitted under the U.S. Copyright Act of 1976, no part of this publication may be reproduced, stored in a retrieval system, or transmitted in any form or by any means electronic, mechanical, photocopying, recording, or otherwise without the written permission of the publisher. For information regarding permissions, send a query to midorianzaimanga@gmail.com.

ISBN (Paperback): 979-8-218-10690-4

Visit the author at www.midorianzai.com

SLIDE

MOM! KATASHI, TERU, SHO!

IT'S SNOWING!

YUKI-DARUMA! LET'S MAKE YUKI-DARUMA!

WAA-

YEAH!

IT'S SNOWING!?

I THOUGHT IT FELT COLD WHEN WE ALL WOKE UP THIS MORNING!

WAIT FOR ME!

MOMMY! COME PLAY WITH US!
IT MUST HAVE STARTED LAST NIGHT.
AT LEAST WE HAVE ENOUGH FIREWOOD FOR THE WINTER.
YES! MOM!
MOM
AND THE REST OF YOU AREN'T GOING OUTSIDE WITHOUT ONE.
YES!
FIRST, LET'S FIND YOUR HAORI.
NOT SALT FARMERS.
SAMURAI, SEIJIRO.
DON'T SAMURAI TRAIN SHIRTLESS IN THE SNOW?
I GOT MY HAORI HERE!

RACE YOU TO THE TOP OF THE HILL, TERU!
OH, LIKE YOU EVER BEAT ME WHEN WE DO!
NOW, WHERE DID YOU PUT YOUR HAORI, SHO?
LET'S BUILD A MILLION YUKI-DARUMA!
I CAN BEAT YOU! I JUST LET YOU WIN, THAT'S ALL.
IF WE BUILD A MILLION, WE COULD FILL UP ALL OF JAPAN!
YEAH! AND WE CAN BE FRIENDS WITH ALL OF THEM!
FOUR YEAR OLDS?
WAIT...
FOUR YEAR OLDS.

ISN'T SHO
TWELVE
NOW?
FOUR?
SNAPS
OPEN
HUH?
WAS THAT
JUST A
DREAM?
THIS...
WAIT-

THIS ISN'T WHERE I WAS WALKING...
....
WHERE-
LOOK AROUND

STUMBLE

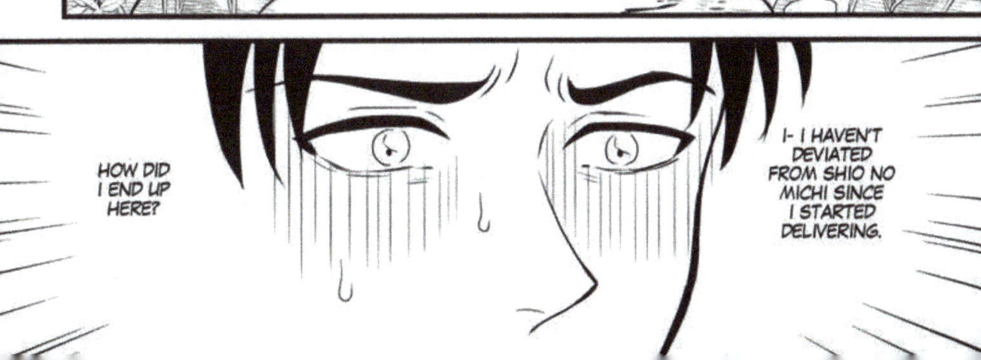

WHERE AM I!?
HOW DID I END UP HERE?
I- I HAVEN'T DEVIATED FROM SHIO NO MICHI SINCE I STARTED DELIVERING.

STEP
...NO!
NOT HERE...
RUSTLE
RUSTLE
NOT HERE EITHER!

MY BOX OF SALT IS MISSING! AND I'M DUE IN MATSUMOTO IN A FEW DAYS!
PANT
PANT
I'VE WALKED THIS ROAD THOUSANDS OF TIMES!
OKAY, SEIJIRO, JUST SETTLE DOWN.
PANICKING ISN'T GOING TO DO YOU ANY GOOD RIGHT NOW.
DEEP BREATH
HOW DID I GET OFF COURSE!? I DON'T EVEN REMEMBER TAKING ANOTHER PATH OR ANYTHING!

DO I STILL HAVE MY MAP?
SEARCH
AT LEAST I STILL HAVE MY SNOWSHOES.
EMPTY
BOTH GONE.
DAMN. MY SALT AND MAP,
THEY MIGHT HAVE TAKEN MY MAP TOO, IF THEY NEEDED TO GET OFF THE MOUNTAIN.
BANDITS MUST HAVE KNOCKED ME OUT AND TAKEN THE SALT.
I THINK IT'S STILL DAYLIGHT. I BETTER GET MOVING BEFORE DUSK COMES.
I CAN'T WORRY ABOUT THAT NOW THOUGH.
DAMN HIDEYOSHI-SAMA. IF HE HADN'T LET JUST THE SAMURAI HAVE THE SWORDS,
I MIGHT HAVE BEEN ABLE TO DEFEND MYSELF!

THIS PROBABLY WOULDN'T BE SO UNNERVING IF I COULD REMEMBER HOW I GOT HERE...

I REALLY HOPE THERE IS A VILLAGE SOMEWHERE CLOSE.
IT'S SO COLD!
RUSTLE

I KNOW I PASSED THAT RICE PADDY.

URGH! WHY IS EVERYTHING SO FOGGY RIGHT NOW?
I DON'T EVEN REMEMBER GETTING HIT IN THE HEAD OR ANYTHING!
DID I PASS ANY SHRINES OR OTHER LANDMARKS? DID I SEE ANYBODY?
BUT I DON'T THINK I LIKE BEING ALONE AND LOST.
AH!
BLOW WARM AIR
...I DON'T MIND TRAVELING ALONE,
OH! AT LEAST THERE'S A FRIENDLY FACE!
A CLEARING?

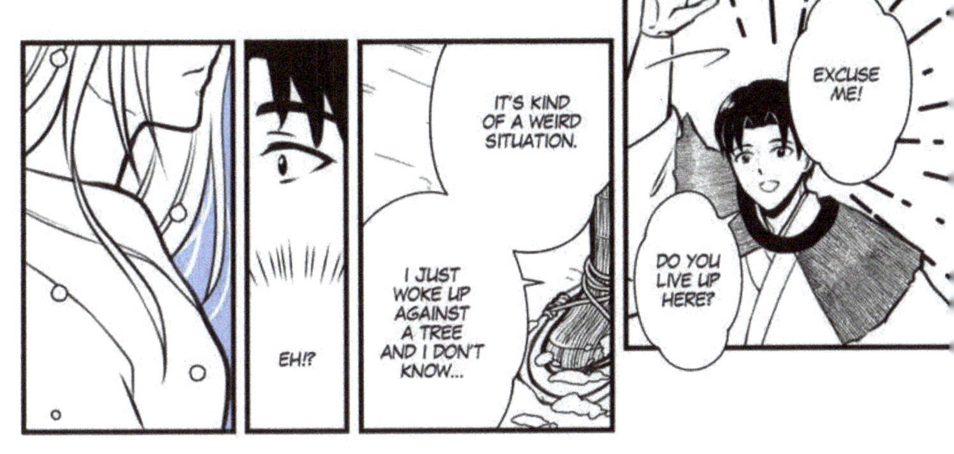

EXCUSE ME!
DO YOU LIVE UP HERE?
IT'S KIND OF A WEIRD SITUATION.
I JUST WOKE UP AGAINST A TREE AND I DON'T KNOW...
EH!?

SHE ONLY WEARS A THIN KIMONO?
Y-YOU'VE GOT TO BE FREEZING!
TAKE OFF
WHERE DID YOU COME FR-
PLEASE TAKE THIS. IT WILL KEEP YOU WARM.
GRAB!
AAH!!
KHH
DROP

!!
C-COLD!
AH...
SEIZE
I...IMPOSSIBLE!
NO...
THE YUKI-ONNA!?

KJRUH
HNGH!
!
FWHH
PULL

NO FOOT-PRINTS...

H-HOW?
FLIP
AH-
SEIJIRO...
AAAAAAAAHHHHH!

I'D HEARD STORIES, BUT I DIDN'T THINK THEY WERE TRUE!
THE YUKI-ONNA...
EVERYWHERE I GO ON SHIO NO MICHI, HER STORY IS DIFFERENT.

A MAN I TRADED SALT WITH ONCE SAID SHE WAS A YUREI WHO PERISHED IN THE SNOW.

I'VE HEARD GOSSIPERS IN VILLAGES I'VE DELIVERED TO SAY SHE WAS JUST ANOTHER YOKAI.

STEP

THUD

OTHERS SAY SHE HAS A CHILD WITH HER...

THERE'S NO END TO HER ORIGINS.

AND I DEFINITELY DON'T WANT TO KNOW WHICH STORY IS CORRECT!

OVER THERE...
AH!
I CAN HIDE UNDER THAT ROCK FORMATION!
SPEED UP

SHE'S HERE!
!!
TREMBLE
TREMBLE
STOP
?
SHE'S WALKING PAST?
!
HOW?
SEIJIRO?

SHE DIDN'T COME LOOKING DOWN HERE...
DUST
OFF
I GOT AWAY...
SEIJIRO.
......
WIND BLOW
COLD
SHE KNOWS ME SOMEHOW.
SHE'LL PROBABLY KEEP CHASING ME UNTIL I'M DEAD.
SHE CALLED MY NAME TWICE.
DID I KNOW HER?

HOW DOES SHE KNOW WHO I AM THOUGH?
I DON'T RECALL STAINING ANYBODY'S HONOR...
I'M GONNA NEED MY MINO IF I'M GONNA SURVIVE OUT HERE.

THERE IT IS!

FLAP

THAT'S BETTER.
PUT ON

WHAT WOULD BE GREAT IS IF I COULD FIGURE OUT HOW I GOT HERE.
MAYBE I COULD FIND A WAY BACK.
STOP
CONCENTRATE...
THAT'S RIGHT.
RUMBLING
RUMBLING

A SMALL SHRINE?
I'LL PAY MY RESPECTS BEFORE I GO.

TIME TO GET BACK ON THE ROAD.

PROBLEM IS,
WHICH WAY DO I GO?

MAYBE IF I CAN GET BACK TO THE VILLAGE, I CAN FIND THE REST OF THE WAY HOME.

I REMEMBER PRAYING AT A SHRINE.
I MUST HAVE WOUND UP IN THE FOREST AFTER I LEFT.

DID IT GET DARKER JUST NOW?
THE SUN WON'T STAY UP FOREVER.
I BETTER FIND SHELTER, AND SOON.
KH
KH
KH

HOW FAR DOES THIS FOREST GO?
I'VE SEEN NOTHING BUT TREES FOR KILOMETERS!
SNATCH
PANTING
I WENT TO THE VILLAGE...
THANK YOU FOR TRADING!
THANK YOU TOO!

THEN I PASSED THAT RICE PADDY I ALWAYS DO WHEN I GO DELIVERING SALT...

...A PERSON?
A SHRINE? A BUILDING?
DID I PASS ANYTHING ELSE BEFORE I WOKE UP?

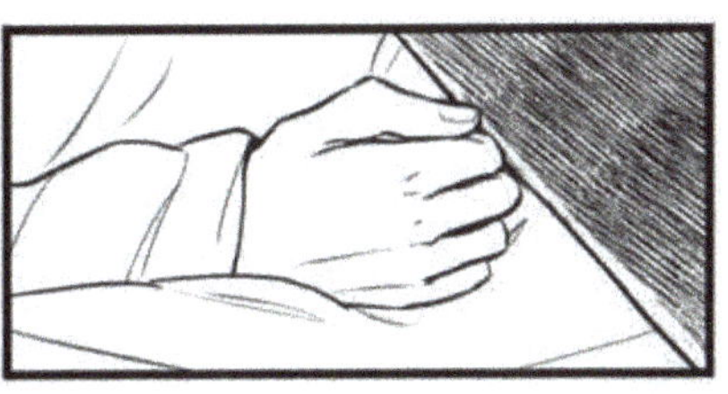

THUD

I'D FEEL A LOT BETTER IF I WASN'T COMPLETELY ALONE UP HERE...
THUD
THUD

SOME PEOPLE FISH FOR WAKASAGI THROUGH ICE. IS THIS SAFE TO CROSS?
BMM
BMM
THIS LAKE...
FEELS THICK ENOUGH.

DEFINITELY DON'T WANT TO KNOW WHAT'S UNDER THERE RIGHT NOW.
KEEP MOVING
SOMETHING IS UNDERNEATH THE ICE!
!
NGH! COLD!
NEVER THOUGHT I'D EVER HAVE TO CROSS A FROZEN LAKE WHILE BEING HUNTED BY A YUKI-ONNA.
FATHER HAD NO REASON TO PREPARE ME FOR THIS.
WHEN HE FELL ILL, HE SUSPECTED HIS TIME WAS COMING.
SO HE QUICKLY TAUGHT ME EVERYTHING I NEEDED TO KNOW ABOUT RUNNING THE SALT FARM.

MOTHER FOLLOWED HIM JUST MONTHS LATER.
BUT I PROMISED HIM I WOULD DO MY ABSOLUTE BEST TO HONOR HIM THROUGH THE SALT FARM.
ONCE FATHER PASSED, I WAS IN CHARGE AT ONLY SIXTEEN YEARS OLD.
IT WAS HARD, HAVING TO FILL IN FOR BOTH PARENTS SO YOUNG.
I WAS FAR FROM PERFECT.
AND I PROMISED HER I WOULD RAISE MY BROTHERS TO BE HONORABLE SALT FARMERS AND MERCHANTS.
HOWEVER, I MANAGED TO KEEP MY PROMISES TO MOTHER.

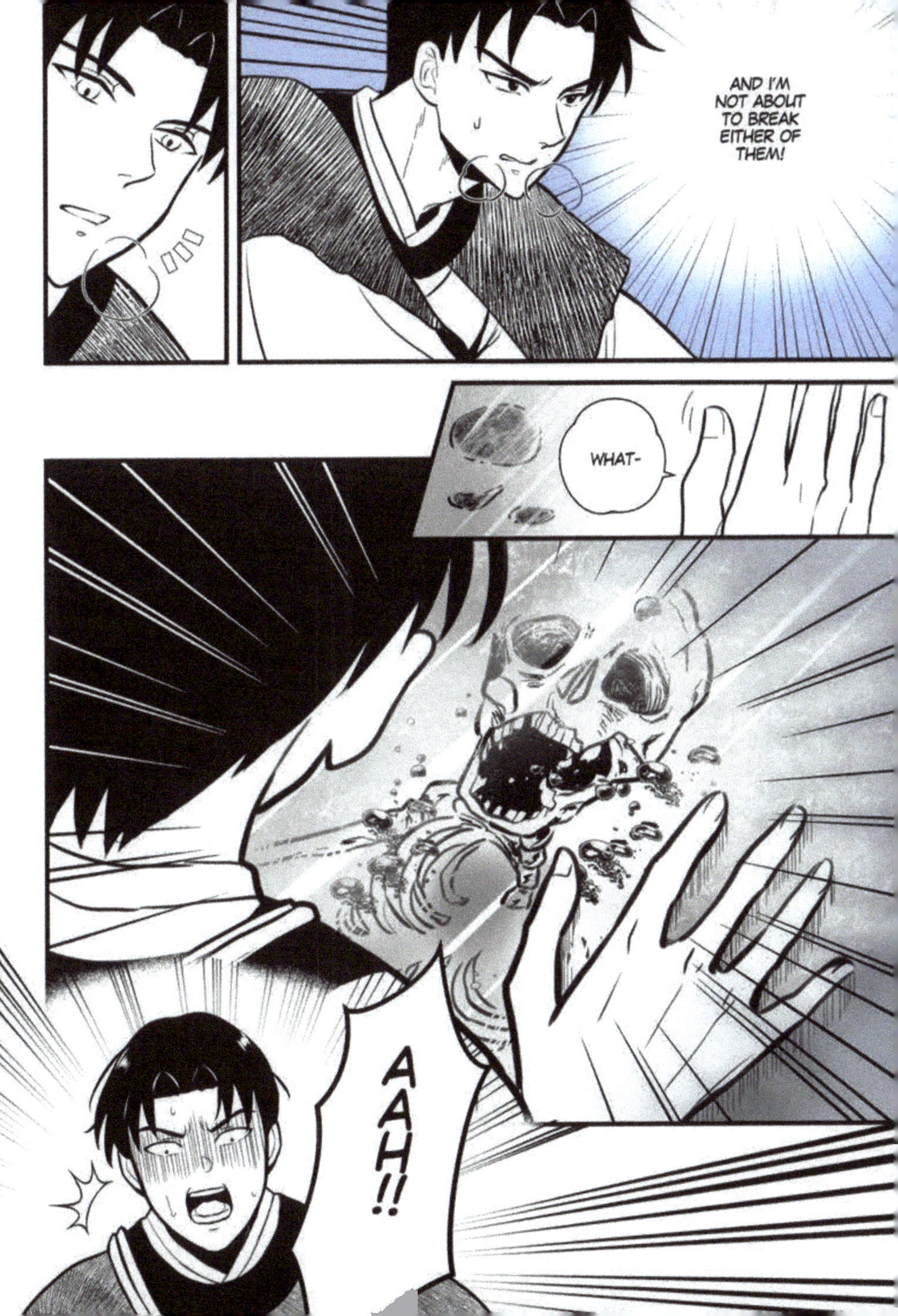
AND I'M NOT ABOUT TO BREAK EITHER OF THEM!
WHAT-
AAH!!

SPEED UP
WHAT WAS THAT!?
GRGH!
HAH...
HAH
THUD
FINALLY! LAND!

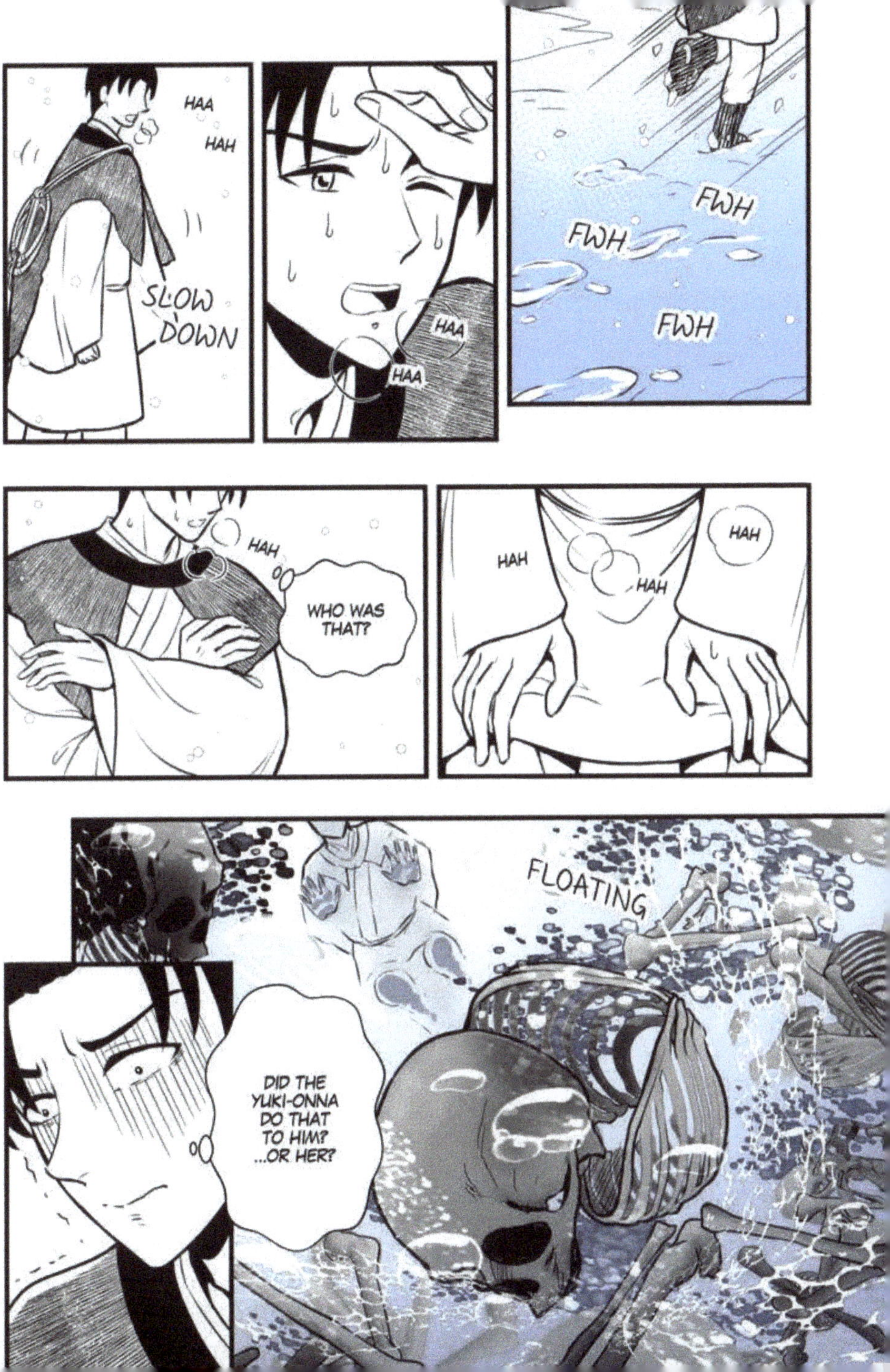

HAA
HAH
SLOW DOWN

HAA
HAA

FWH
FWH
FWH

HAH
WHO WAS THAT?

HAH
HAH
HAH

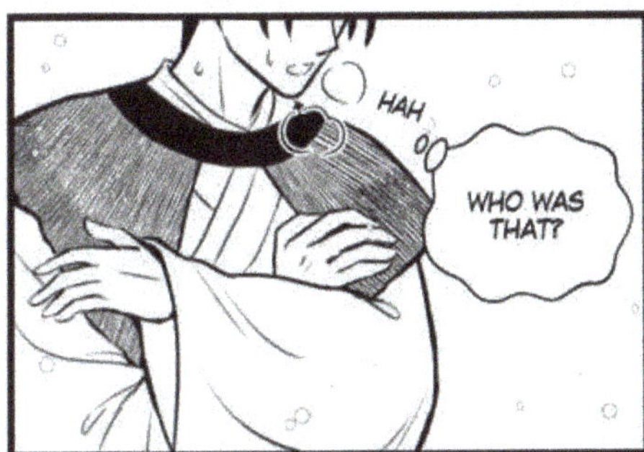

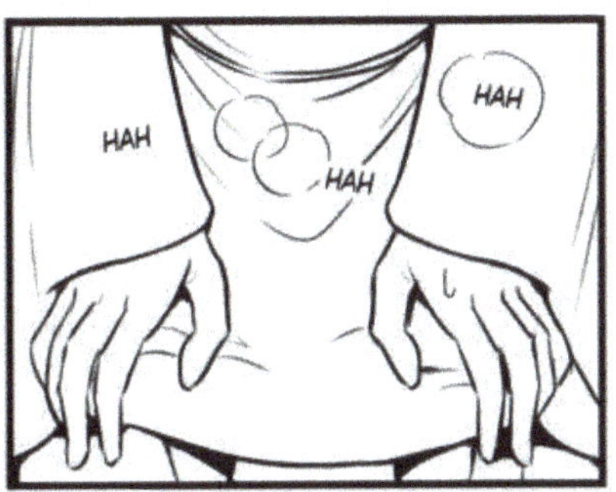

FLOATING

DID THE YUKI-ONNA DO THAT TO HIM? ...OR HER?

...ALONE?

WERE THEY...

DO THEY HAVE FAMILY WONDERING WHERE THEY ARE?
WORRYING ABOUT THEM?

AH! GOOD!

BUT I KNOW I'M GONNA END UP LIKE THAT PERSON IF I STAY UP HERE!

I DON'T KNOW THE ANSWERS TO ANY OF THOSE QUESTIONS,

IF I JUST KEEP GOING,
I CAN AT LEAST GET CLOSER TO THE BASE OF THE MOUNTAIN BEFORE NIGHTFALL.
LOOKS LIKE I'M GOING DOWN.
DOWN IS WHAT WE WANT.
A FLAT LAND...
!?

HEY!
YUKI-DARUMA!
IS ANYONE HERE?
HELLO?
THERE'S PROBABLY PEOPLE UP HERE!
...IS ANYBODY HERE!?
HELLO?

AND JUST NEED A WAY TO GET-
PULL
I GOT LOST UP HERE,
GRAB
SLIDE
SLIDE
YOU'RE HERE...

TUG
TUG
NGH!
AGH!
THE YUKI-DARUMA!?
CRASH!
NGH!!
AA-
AAHHH!!

SEIJIRO...
YOU DON'T REMEMBER?
NO, I DON'T!
WHO ARE YOU!? WHAT DO YOU WANT FROM ME!?
WHY ARE YOU CHASING ME!?

FLOAT
....
SMILE
OKAY, FORGET REASONING!

SNOWFALL

I'VE GOT TO LOSE HER,
BUT THERE DON'T APPEAR TO BE ANY ROCK FORMATIONS OR TREES I CAN CLIMB!
DID SHE GET FASTER!?
SPEED UP

AAH!

THERE'S NO TIME!

FUU

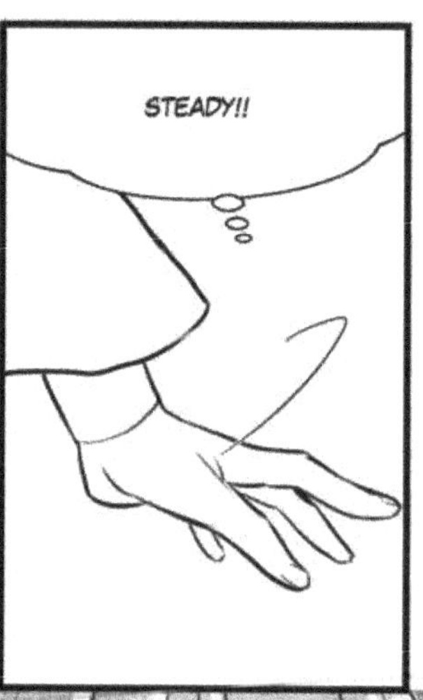

STEADY!!

STOPPING MEANS DEATH!

THUD
THUD
THUD
STOP
HAH...!

DAMN! THE SUN'S DOWN!

FWOOSH
FWOOSH
SEIJIRO...

I'M NOT SURE WHAT I DID...
TO MAKE YOU WANT TO KILL ME...
STARE
BUT I'M NOT GOING TO GIVE YOU THE CHANCE!

JUST GOTTA
KEEP GOING...!

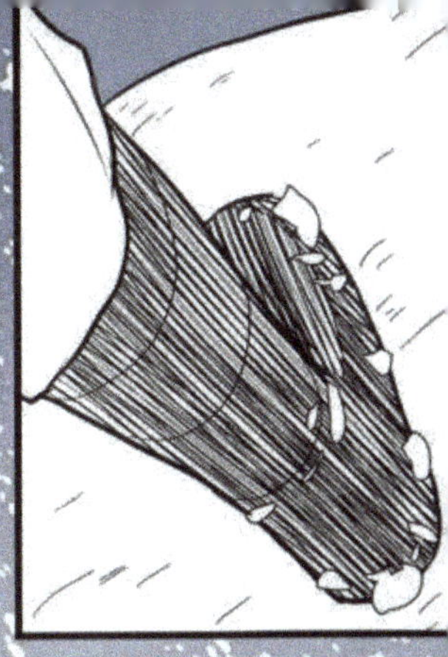

WHAT!?

YOU'RE NOT GOING TO DIE UNTIL YOU'RE AN OLD MAN,
SURROUNDED BY YOUR FAMILY AND A FIRE BURNING UNDER THE SALT POT!
!!
HOW DID SHE CATCH UP SO FAST!?
FOCUS!
SPEED UP
JUST KEEP RUNNING!

GRAB
THAT WAS CLOSE!
BREAK
BREAK
WAH!
SLIP

UGH...
FHHHHH
AH!
KH
KH
UNF!
SLIDE
!!

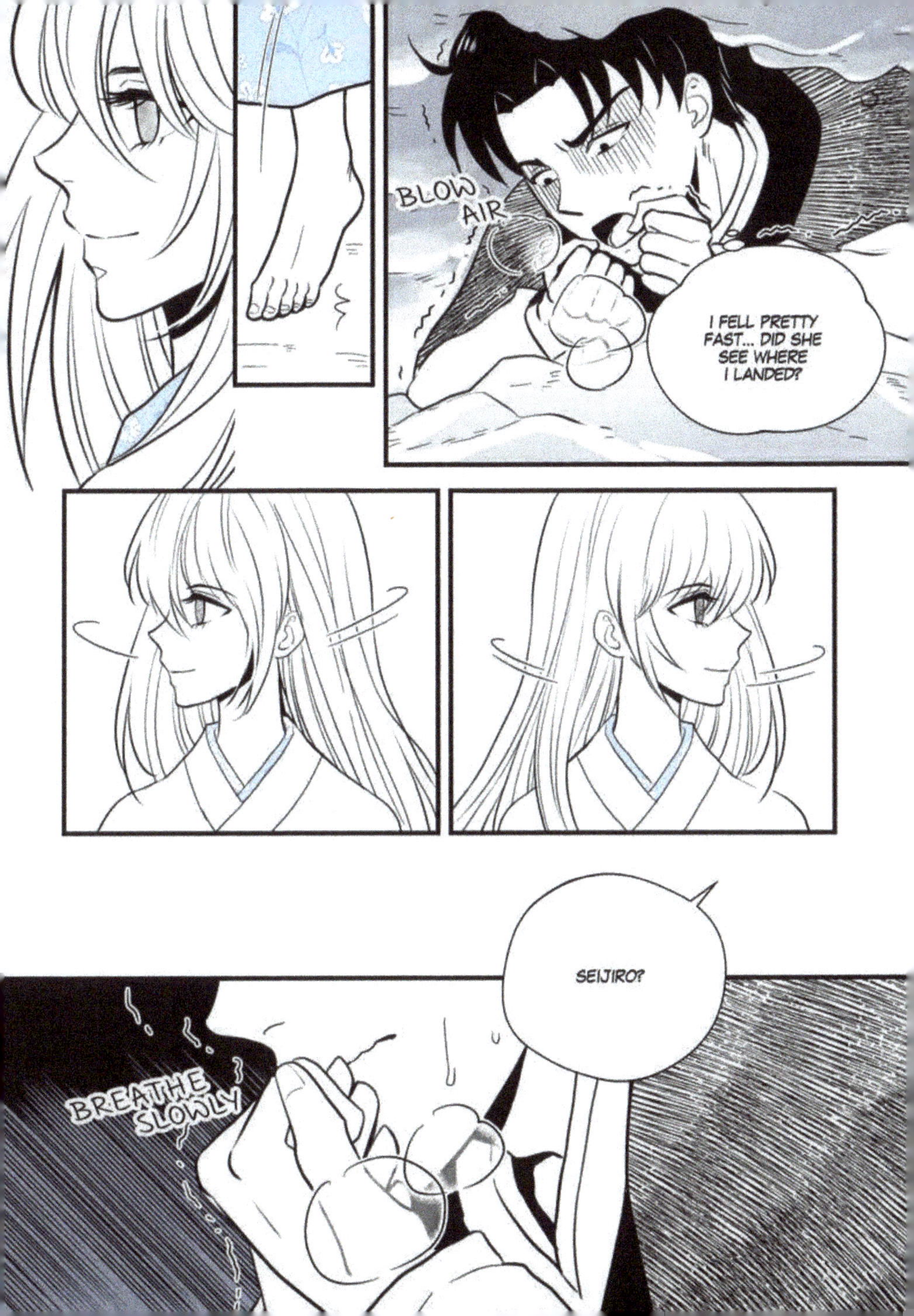

BLOW AIR
I FELL PRETTY FAST... DID SHE SEE WHERE I LANDED?
SEIJIRO?
BREATHE SLOWLY

SEIJIRO?

....
I'M... I'M SAFE?

BRUSHING
SNOW
CLIMBING
OUT

...SHE'S OUT THERE, I DON'T KNOW IF I'LL EVER FEEL SAFE.
BUT AS LONG AS...
I JUST WANT TO GO HOME AND BE WITH MY FAMILY.
IT'S HARDER TO WALK WITHOUT MY SNOWSHOES.
THAT'S ALL I WANT.

I'VE HEARD HEAT WILL CAUSE HER TO EVAPORATE INTO THIN AIR.
CRUNCH
CRUNCH
ENTRANCE OF ANOTHER FOREST...
AH!
IF I CAN GET A FIRE GOING, MAYBE SHE'LL FINALLY LEAVE ME ALONE.

CRUNCH
CRUNCH
HAVE I BEEN HERE BEFORE?
HUH...
THIS FEELS FAMILIAR.

AH! PERFECT!

IT WON'T BE A BIG FIRE, BUT THIS MIGHT MAKE ENOUGH TO STAY WARM FOR A WHILE.

IT'S HARD TO SEE IN THIS FOREST. AT LEAST I CAN START A FIRE WITH JUST A COUPLE OF STICKS.

CLATTER
CLATTER
I'LL JUST SET IT UP HERE.
IT'S GETTING SO DARK IN HERE, I DON'T KNOW IF I'LL EVEN HAVE A FIELD OF VISION SOON WITHOUT THE FIRE.

JUST GOTTA TRY TO GET AN EMBER-

?

IS THAT...
OO
WHAT THE-!?
BLOOD!?
DROP
HUH!?

QUIET
IS SHE-!?
SEIJIRO...
!!
HUH...!?
BACK UP
WHAT'S GOING ON?
QUIET

EMPTY
SEIJIRO...
!?
WHAT DID I EVER DO TO YOU!?
WHO ARE YOU!?
YOU KNOW WHAT'S HAPPENING.

BACK UP

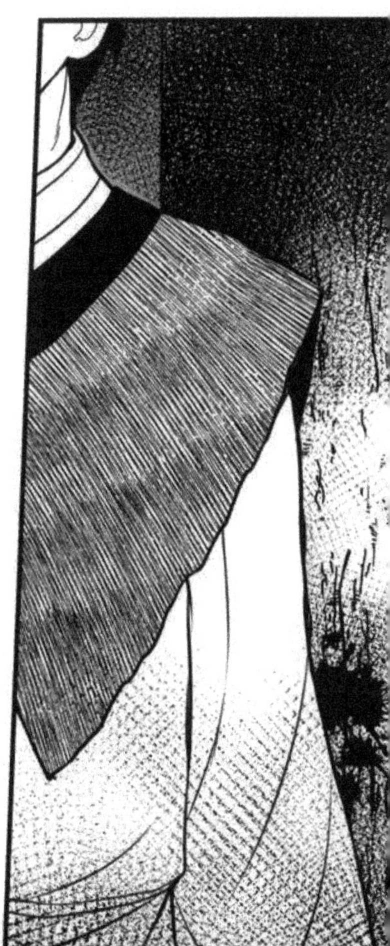

WHY WON'T YOU LEAVE ME ALONE!?

SEIJIRO... YOU REALLY DON'T REMEMBER, DO YOU?
REMEMBER WHAT...?

IT ONLY HAPPENED JUST A FEW MINUTES AGO.

YOU MUST NOT REALIZE...

THE BLOOD ON THAT TREE BEHIND YOU...

...IS YOURS.

IS THIS NOT WHERE YOU FIRST WOKE UP?

WHAT!?
W-

HUH!?
MY...
MY MEMORIES...
STEP
STEP

ALL RIGHT. IT'S GOING TO TAKE ME A FEW DAYS BEFORE I REACH MATSUMOTO.
I'LL HAVE TO FIND AN INN ALONG THE WAY.
STEP
STEP
I HOPE MY BROTHERS ARE OKAY.
WHAT I WOULD GIVE TO BE BACK HOME WITH THEM RIGHT NOW...
STEP

BUT WALKING THROUGH KAMIKOCHI IS ALWAYS SUCH A BEAUTIFUL TREK.
CREAK
JUST SO THEY CAN-
MAYBE WHEN TERU OR SHO ARE OLD ENOUGH,
I'LL TAKE THEM WITH ME ON SHIO NO MICHI,
AH-!?

HAHH...!
AH!
GRAB
SLIP
AAAAAAHHHHH!!!
SLIP
NO!!

NO!
AAAAAAHH!!

CRACK
AGH!!
SNAP
SPLINTER
MY BONES BREAK,
MY SALT GOES FLYING EVERYWHERE...

CRACK
BOUNCE

CRUNCH
BOUNCE

N...
NO...
I REMEMBER NOW...
EVERYTHING!
TREMBLE
PLEASE! I CAN'T DIE!
NOT YET!
YOU'RE DYING, SEIJIRO.
NO!
I HAVE A FAMILY BACK HOME!
A SALT FARM!
MY BROTHERS ARE WAITING FOR ME!
STEP

SHO!
TERU!
KATASHI!
WRIGGLE
SOMEONE! ANYONE!
HELP!
SEIJIRO...
YOU KNOW I'M NOT HERE.
YOU KNOW NO ONE'S HERE.

IT'S...

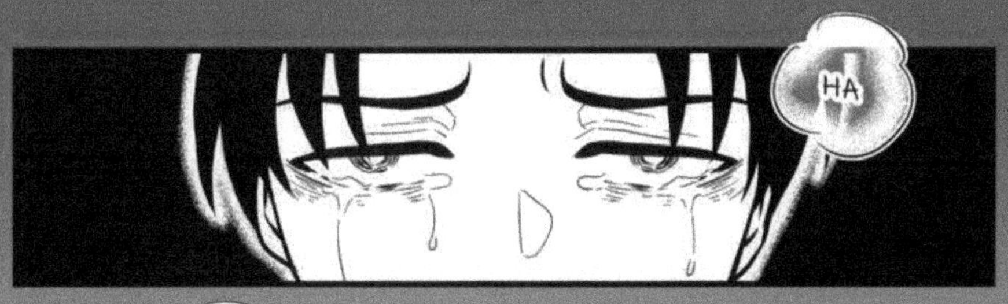

THIS ISN'T HOW
I WANTED...
THIS TO END...

...I DIDN'T
WANT...
TO DIE
HERE...

...ALONE...

SHE IS COMING - END

she is
coming

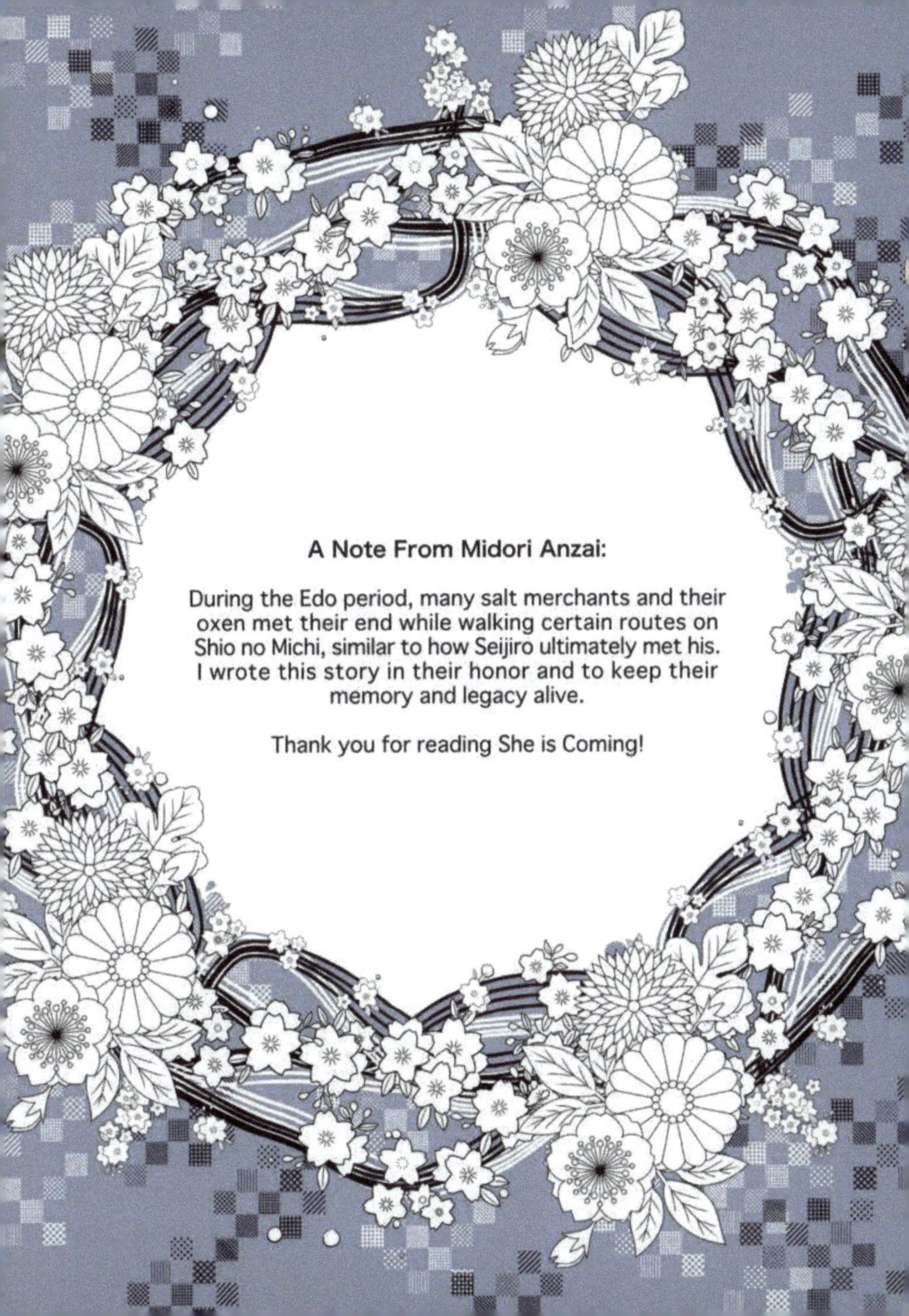

A Note From Midori Anzai:

During the Edo period, many salt merchants and their oxen met their end while walking certain routes on Shio no Michi, similar to how Seijiro ultimately met his. I wrote this story in their honor and to keep their memory and legacy alive.

Thank you for reading She is Coming!

TERMINOLOGY

MINO (PAGE 21)

MADE OF STRAW FOR ITS WATER REPELLENT PROPERTIES, THESE CAPES WERE WORN WHEN TRAVELING IN HEAVY RAIN OR SNOW.

HAORI (PAGE 2)

TRADITIONAL JACKET WORN OVER A KIMONO. DURING THE EDO PERIOD, MEN EXCLUSIVELY WORE THEM. TODAY, BOTH MEN AND WOMEN WEAR HAORIS WHEN THEY WEAR KIMONOS.

SHIO NO MICHI (PAGE 6)

LITERALLY TRANSLATES TO "SALT ROAD". MERCHANTS WOULD TRAVEL SEVERAL PATHS ON SHIO NO MICHI TO TRADE SALT FOR VARIOUS GOODS, INCLUDING (BUT NOT LIMITED TO) FISH AND TOBACCO.

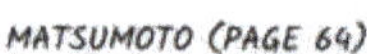

KAMIKOCHI (PAGE 65)

A HIGHLAND IN THE HIDA MOUNTAINS, LOCATED IN THE WESTERN REGION OF THE NAGANO PREFECTURE OF JAPAN.

MATSUMOTO (PAGE 64)

A CITY IN THE NAGANO PREFECTURE OF JAPAN. AS OF MARCH OF 2019, IT HAS A POPULATION OF UNDER 240,000 PEOPLE.

TERMINOLOGY 2

YŪREI (PAGE 17)

A TYPE OF YŌKAI, THEY ARE BELIEVED TO BE THE GHOSTS OF THE DEAD. THEY ARE CAPABLE OF INFLICTING POWERFUL CURSES, AND OFTEN HAUNT A PERSON OR A PLACE.

YŌKAI (PAGE 17)

A SUPERNATURAL CREATURE FROM JAPANESE FOLKLORE. VAST IN THEIR RANGE OF POWERS, APPEARANCE, AND ORIGINS, THEY CONTINUE TO BE A POWERFUL INFLUENCE IN JAPANESE CULTURE TODAY.

YUKI-ONNA (PAGE 13)

A FAMOUS YŌKAI, HER NAME TRANSLATES TO "SNOW WOMAN". SHE HAS DIFFERENT LEGENDS IN DIFFERENT REGIONS OF JAPAN, INCLUDING ONE WHERE SHE MARRIES A MAN AND BEARS CHILDREN WITH HIM. AS SEIJIRO SAYS ON PAGE 17, THE NUMBER OF YUKI-ONNA LEGENDS ARE ALMOST INNUMERABLE.

YUKI-DARUMA (PAGE 3)

THE JAPANESE WORD FOR 'SNOWMAN'. I CHOSE THIS SPECIFIC WORD BECAUSE THESE PARTICULAR SNOWMEN ARE BUILT AFTER DOLLS OF BODHIDARMA, WHO BROUGHT ZEN BUDDHISM FROM CHINA TO INDIA. YUKI-DARUMA HAVE TWO BALLS INSTEAD OF THREE.

MIDORI ANZAI

A fan of anime and manga her whole life, Midori Anzai seeks to bring them both to a wider audience with her own unique style. She is native to the United States, where she resides.

Website: www.midorianzai.com

LIONA

Liona is a manga and doujinshi artist based in Taiwan. She freelances for work and is half of Bear Lion Shop art circle / shop on Etsy. She takes illustration commissions, and occasionally comics.

Website: www.liona.moe

WAIT! THIS IS THE END OF THE BOOK!
HOW TO READ MANGA
START
1
2
3
4
5

www.ingramcontent.com/pod-product-compliance
Lightning Source LLC
Chambersburg PA
CBHW040839010826
48978CB00012BB/823